Dedicated to my children, Preston and Sydney.
You are my life's inspiration.
— TG

To my dear friends Andrea, Ari and Stella.
Also, special thanks to little Samuel
who allowed me to use his drawings in
one scene of the book.
— RA

Your Father Forever

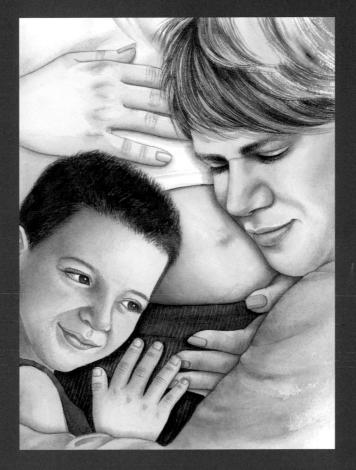

By Travis Griffith ✧ Illustrated by Raquel Abreu

ILLUMINATION Arts

PUBLISHING COMPANY, INC.

Bellevue, Washington

On the day you were born,
I welcomed you into my arms

And knew that
I would love you forever.

From that moment on
I promised to guide you,

As together we explore
the wonders of this world.

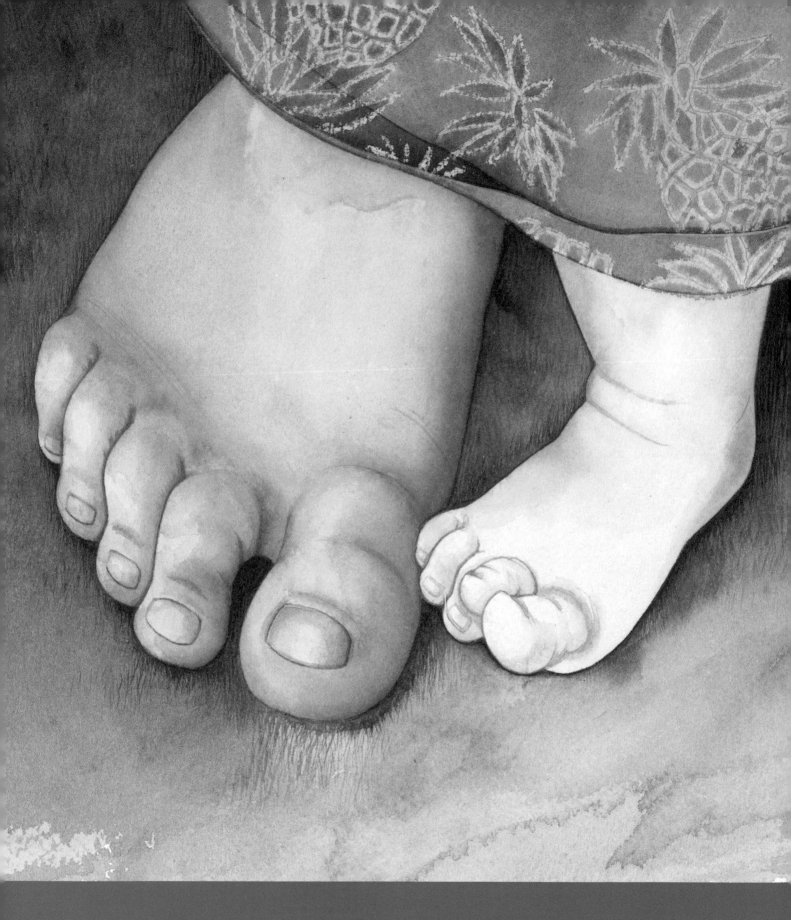

When you take your first steps
and learn to ride your bike,

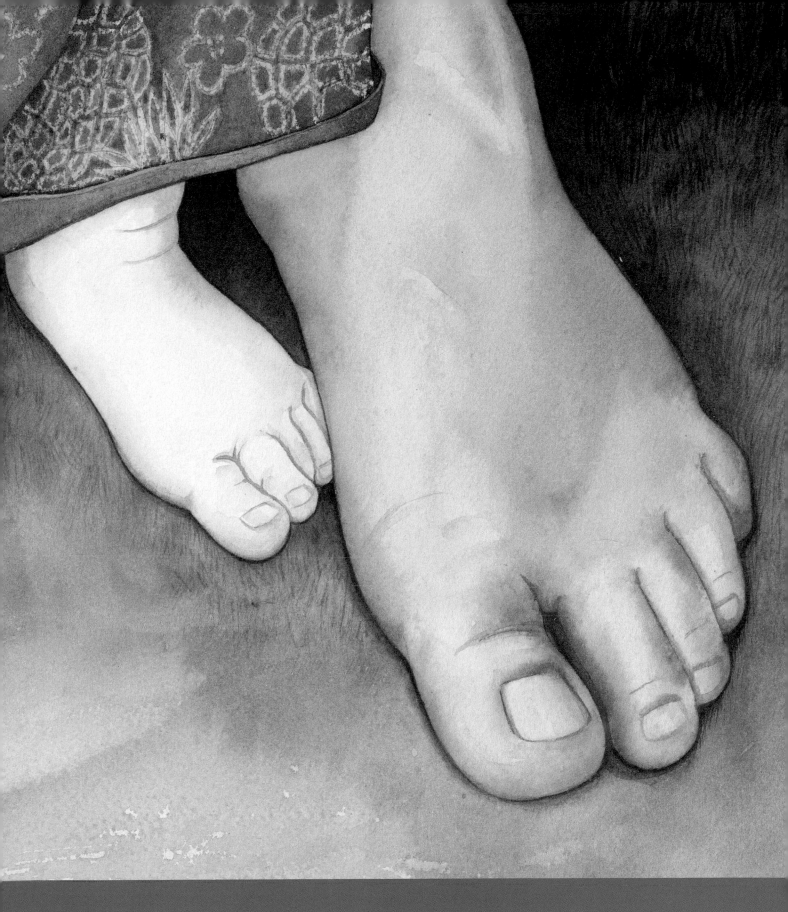

I will be at your side
to help you along.

I will tuck you in at bedtime
and read your favorite stories.

And I'll be there to listen
when you want to read to me.

If you wake during the night
feeling sad or afraid

I'll kiss away your tears
and rock you back to sleep.

I'll wrestle with you on the ground
and toss you into the air

"Again!" and "Again!"
for as long as you want me to.

I will be waiting for you
at the bottom of the slide,

When warm spring days invite us
to play outside.

We will have great fun
and share lots of laughter.

And I'll be there with a hug
when you need to cry.

Your friends will be welcome in our lives
and in our home,

Where every person is valued
and all feelings can be shared.

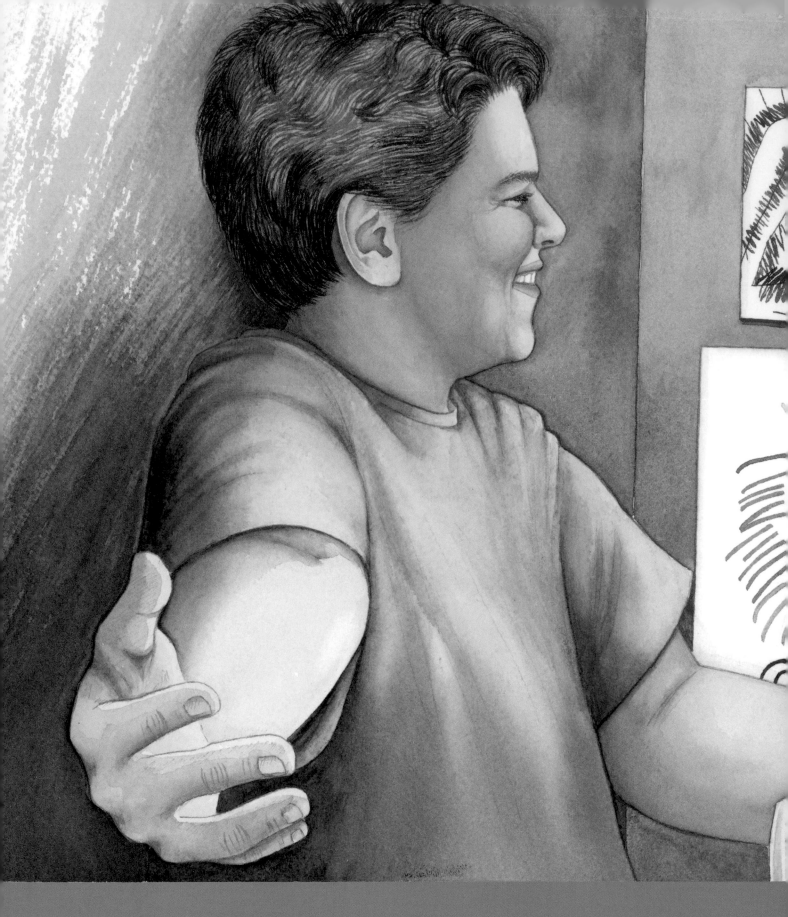

I will help you with your homework
and cheer you on at games.

We'll celebrate each new discovery
as your brilliant life unfolds.

Together we will search for the answers
to all of your questions,

And I will encourage you
to follow the wisdom of your heart.

On warm summer nights
we will search the sky and marvel

At the grandeur of the universe
and all the mysteries beyond.

The cherished memories we create
will help us both to see,

The sparkling celebration of life
that you will forever be.

Though life may lead you
to many far away places,

Our home will always
be waiting here for you.

I will be your daddy
as long as you want me to.

But I will be your father... *forever.*

ILLUMINATION
Arts

Publishing Company, Inc.
P.O. Box 1865, Bellevue, WA 98009
Tel: 425-644-7185 ✧ 888-210-8216 (orders only) ✧ Fax: 425-644-9274
liteinfo@illumin.com ✧ www.illumin.com

Library of Congress Cataloging-in-Publication Data

Griffith, Travis.
 Your father forever / by Travis Griffith ; illustrated by Raquel Abreu.
  p. cm.
 Summary: A devoted father promises to nurture, guide, and protect his
children forever.
 ISBN-13: 978-0-9740190-3-1 (hardcover : alk. paper)
 ISBN-10: 0-9740190-3-8 (hardcover : alk. paper)
 [1. Father and child–Fiction.] I. Abreu, Raquel, ill. II. Title.
 PZ7.G88354You 2005
 [E]–dc22

 2005015611

Publisher's Appreciation: We wish to acknowledge our "outside editing team"—Emma Roberts, Ruth Thompson,
Natasha Cohen and Kim Shealy—for their invaluable assistance in polishing this inspiring offering. —IAI

Published in the United States of America
Printed in Singapore by Tien Wah Press
Book Designer: Molly Murrah, Murrah & Company, Kirkland, WA

Illumination Arts Publishing Company, Inc. is a member of Publisher's in Partnership—
replanting our nation's forests.

More inspiring picture books from Illumination Arts

Little Yellow Pear Tomatoes
Demian Elaine Yumei/Nicole Tamarin, ISBN 0-9740190-2-X
Ponder the never-ending circle of life through the eyes of a young girl, who marvels at all the energy and collaboration it takes to grow yellow pear tomatoes.

Something Special
Terri Cohlene/Doug Keith, ISBN 0-9740190-1-1
A curious little frog finds a mysterious gift outside his home near the castle moat. It's *Something Special*…What can it be?

Am I a Color Too?
Heidi Cole/Nancy Vogl/Gerald Purnell, ISBN 0-9740190-5-4
A young interracial boy wonders why people are labeled by the color of their skin. Seeing that people dream, feel, sing, dance and love regardless of their color, he asks, "Am I a color, too?"

The Tree
Dana Lyons/David Danioth, ISBN 0-9701907-1-9
An urgent call to preserve our fragile environment, *The Tree* reminds us that hope for a brighter future lies in our own hands.

Too Many Murkles
Heidi Charissa Schmidt/Mary Gregg Byrne, ISBN 0-9701907-7-8
Each spring the people of Summerville gather to prevent the dreaded Murkles from entering their village. Unfortunately, this year there are more of the strange, smelly creatures than ever.

We Share One World
Jane E. Hoffelt/Marty Husted, ISBN 0-9701907-8-6
Wherever we live—whether we work in the fields, the waterways, the mountains or the cities—all people and creatures share one world.

In Every Moon There Is A Face
Charles Mathes/Arlene Graston, ISBN 0-9701907-4-3
On this magical voyage of discovery and delight, children of all ages connect with their deepest creative selves.

A Mother's Promise
Lisa Humphrey/David Danioth ISBN 0-9701907-9-4
A lifetime of sharing begins with the sacred vow a woman makes to her unborn child.

To view our whole collection visit us at www.illumin.com